First published in 2012
by Hodder Children's Books

This edition published in 2017

Text and illustrations copyright © Mick Inkpen 2012

Hodder Children's Books
An imprint of Hachette Children's Group
Part of Hodder & Stoughton
Carmelite House, 50 Victoria Embankment
London EC4Y 0DZ

The right of Mick Inkpen to be identified as the author
and illustrator of this Work has been asserted by him in
accordance with the Copyright, Designs and Patents Act 1988.

A catalogue record of this book is available from the British Library.

ISBN: 978 1 444 93126 6

10 9 8 7 6 5 4 3 2 1

Printed in China

An Hachette UK Company
www.hachette.co.uk

FSC
www.fsc.org
MIX
Paper from
responsible sources
FSC® C104740

Wibbly Pig

picks a pet

h

*Hodder
Children's
Books*

'Guess what!' says Wibbly Pig. 'Big Pig's sister's friend is getting a new pet today!'

It is true. Big Pig's sister's friend is off to the

...et shop with her pocket money.

'What do you think she'll choose?' says Scruffy Pig. 'I bet it will be something boring. Something really boring, like a hamster. . .

or a goldfish. . .

or a rabbit!

Yes, that's what she'll choose, a **rabbit!**'

'Oh no, not a **rabbit!**'

'If you could choose,' says Wibbly Pig. 'If you could choose anything, anything at all, what would YOU choose?'

'Anything at all?' says Scruffy Pig.

'Anything,
except a rabbit.'

'I'd choose an
elephant!
We could have
a water fight
with an elephant!

You can't
do that with
a rabbit!'

'I'd have a bear!
Bears are best.
Especially polar bears!
Much better than
a rabbit!'

'It would be
cool to have a
kangaroo!

Tiny Pig could
go for a ride
in the pouch!

You can't do that
with a rabbit!'

'We could have giraffes!
We could see for miles on a giraffe!'

'You can't do that with a rabbit either.'

'Or what about a dolphin!'

wheeeeeeeeeeeeeeeeeeee

'I bet she won't choose anything like this!' says Scruffy Pig.

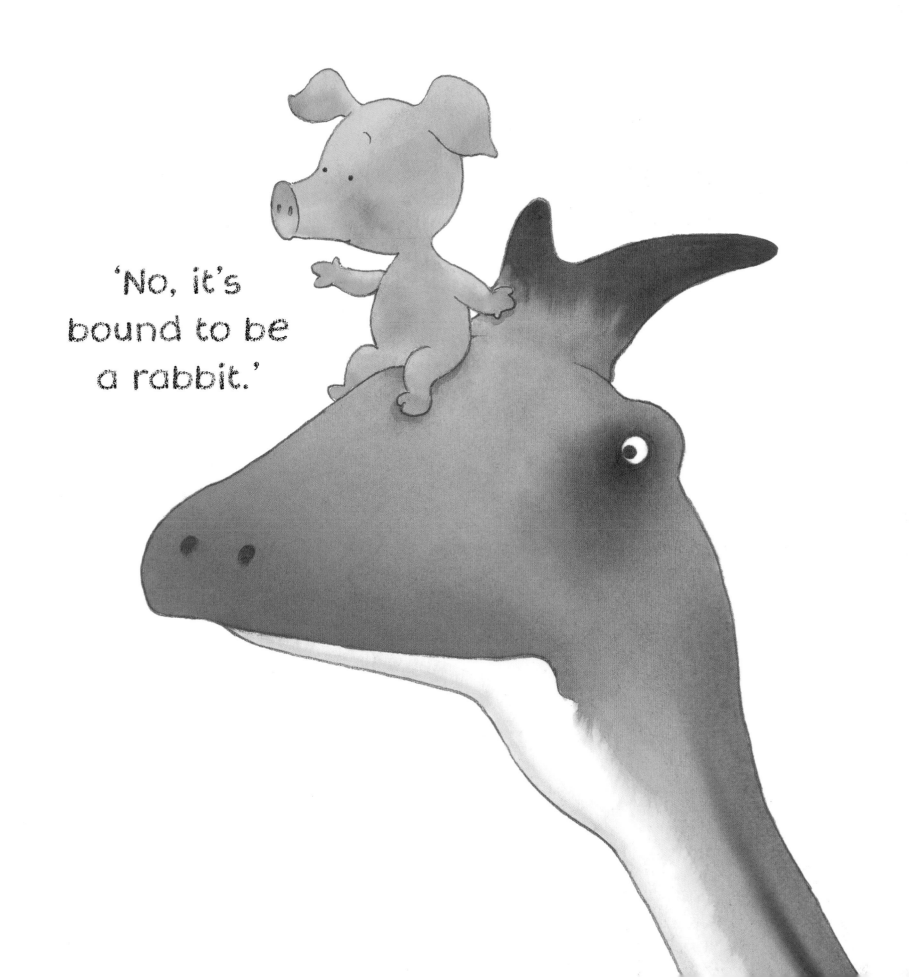

'No, it's
bound to be
a rabbit.'

And sure enough,
when Big Pig's sister's
friend comes back from
the pet shop she has a large,
brown and white. . .

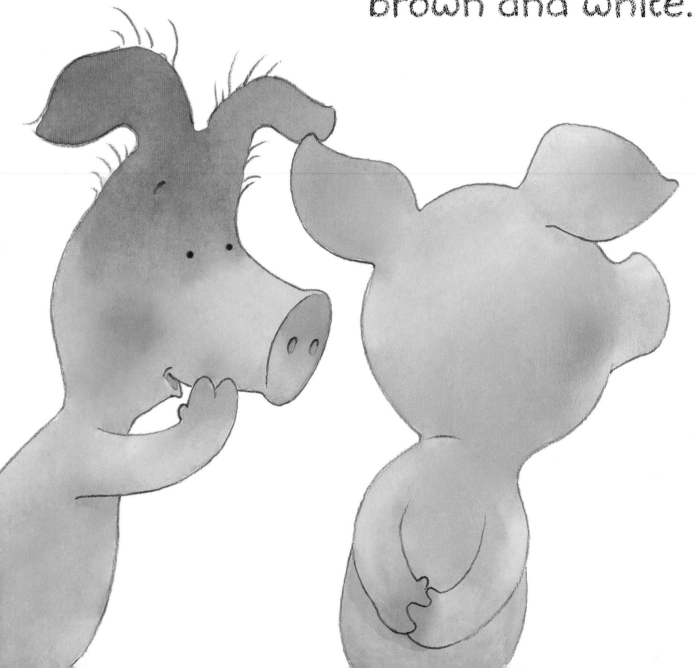

. . . .rabbit.

'Thought so,'
says Wibbly Pig.

'Boring!' whispers
Scruffy Pig.

But,
the rabbit hops onto
Scruffy Pig's lap.
It licks his face.

(He forgets about the elephant.)

Then it licks Wibbly.

(He forgets about the polar bear and the kangaroo.)

The rabbit cleans its ears.

(They forget
all about the giraffe,
the dolphin
and the dinosaurs.)

The rabbit runs three times
round Wibbly Pig and thumps
the floor with its foot.
Thump!
Thump!
Thump!

'How much do
rabbits cost?' says
Wibbly Pig.

'It's really cute!'
says Scruffy Pig.

'Yes it is!'
says Big Pig's sister's
friend, very proudly. . .

'And he can do
two kinds
of poo,
too!'

Great Kipper books
to share together

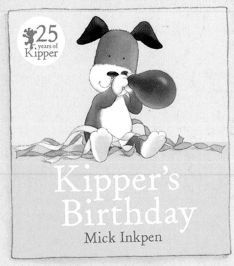

Kipper's
Birthday

Mick Inkpen

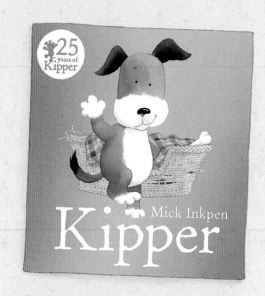

Mick Inkpen

Kipper

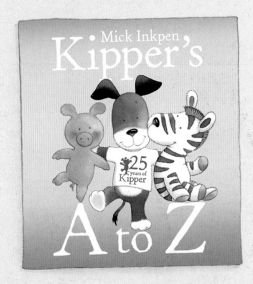

Mick Inkpen
Kipper's

A to Z

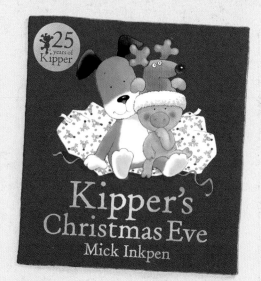

Kipper's
Christmas Eve
Mick Inkpen